THE
CHURCH MICE
IN ACTION

A TEMPLAR BOOK

This edition published in the UK in 2011 by Templar Publishing,
an imprint of The Templar Company Limited,
The Granary, North Street, Dorking, Surrey, RH4 1DN, UK
www.templarco.co.uk

First published in the UK in 1982 by Macmillan

Copyright © 1982 by Graham Oakley

1 3 5 7 9 10 8 6 4 2

ISBN 978-1-84877-077-5

Printed in China

THE
CHURCH MICE
IN ACTION

GRAHAM OAKLEY

templar publishing

MODERN CLASSICS

ONE DAY, quite late in the summer, the church mice
and Sampson the church cat were taking it easy in the churchyard.

They were in a really mellow mood. But then Humphrey,
who was a bit of a pessimist, said through a mouthful of blackberry
that late summer was almost early winter and as the vestry roof
was as leaky as ever the near future looked pretty wet and shivery.

Somehow the mood wasn't quite as mellow after that.

There were two other people in the churchyard.
One was the parson and the other was his sister who was
spending a couple of weeks with him.

The parson was telling his sister all about
squinch arches and crockets and things and she
was telling him all about her best friend's new
hat when suddenly she saw Sampson.

Sampson was dreaming about the lovely times
he used to have before he took his vow never to catch mice
when a strange noise woke him up. It sounded something
like, "Whoooose a booooooooooooooooooootiful
puddy tat den. Come to mummmmy."
He opened his eyes and saw an awesome sight.

"Roderick dear, he simply must come and stay
at the vicarage," the parson's sister said to the parson.

And without more ado she carried Sampson off.

Next morning Arthur and Humphrey went across to the vicarage just to make sure that Sampson was all right

and they were pleased to find that he was being looked after very, very well indeed.

After that they went back to the churchyard and joined the other mice who were breakfasting on something lovely that had been thrown over the wall during the night. Arthur was on his third chip when his eye fell on the ad. The idea it gave him was so brilliant that he had to swallow two more chips very quickly to calm his nerves. Then he informed Humphrey that the vestry roof problem was solved once and for all.

Humphrey only really liked ideas he'd thought of himself so he looked very doubtful and said that
Sampson couldn't win anything except booby prizes. Arthur said that that was true as far as
Handsomeness and Cleverness were concerned but after what they had seen at the vicarage
he thought Sampson would knock spots off anyone in the well-groomed department.
Humphrey just grunted but he agreed to write the letter to the parson's sister explaining the plan
because only he knew the correct way of addressing important people.

The parson's sister was a bit put out at being written to by a pack of mice but the parson made her see reason.
He said that if he relied on the charity of his fellow men the vestry roof wouldn't be mended until the middle
of the twenty-third century, so why not give the mice a chance?

So Sampson was entered for the Best Groomed Cat prize. The mice hadn't intended
to come on the day, because of the number of cats present but Humphrey worked
out a plan to make certain that Sampson won and they had to be there to carry it out.
Arthur had objected, using words like "un-sporting" and "downright un-British", but Humphrey had
stood up for his plan, saying things about "mealy-mouthed hypocrites" and "nambypamby do-gooders".

The mayor opened the cat show with a little speech. He begun by saying that since the time of Dick Whittington
mayors and cats had gone together like fish and chips and the only reason why he didn't have a cat himself
was because his wife was frightened of getting cat fleas in her fur coats.
He ended by patting the first contestant on the head.

Or rather he would have done
if the mice hadn't put their plan into operation.

The plan was very simple, though it called for
the most steely-nerved of the mice to carry it out.

And the plan's success depended on Sampson doing absolutely nothing.
He did it perfectly.

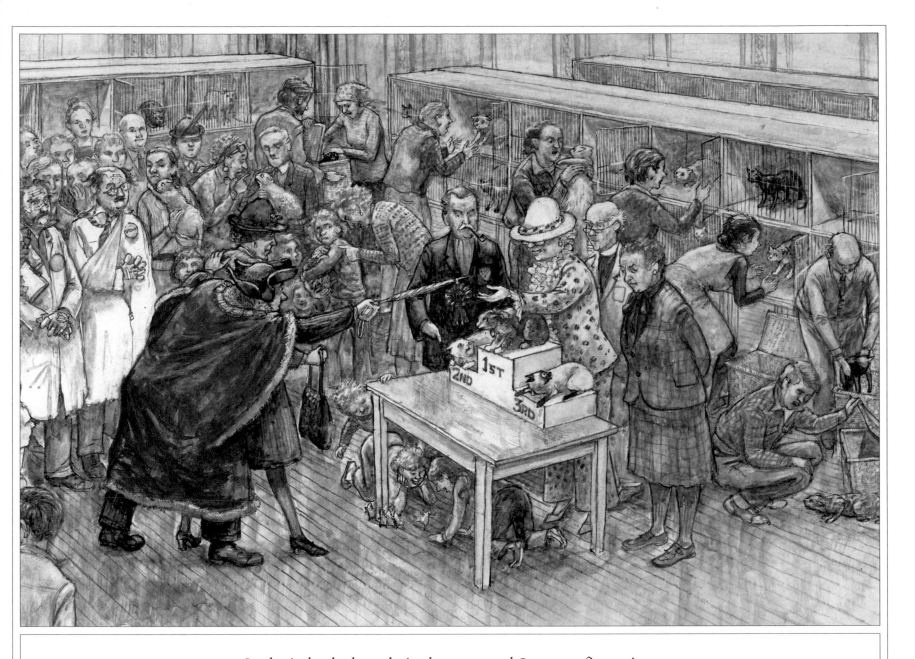

So the judge had no choice but to award Sampson first prize.
The mayor presented the prizes and he had intended to make another speech but he didn't because
the only words that came into his head were things like "devilish fiends", "furies from Hell" and "ravaging beasts"
and he didn't really think that would make him very popular with cat-loving voters.

After his success Sampson was entered in other cat shows and, with the aid of the mice, his prizes soon amounted to ten pounds, a year's supply of cat litter and three dozen boxes of flea powder. Humphrey claimed all the credit. "Chaps like me," he said, "just stick our hands in the World's Pocket and take what we want." Arthur said he supposed you *could* describe swindling honest folk like that. All the other mice just called him a ninny.
Next morning there was an article about Sampson in the paper.

The mice read it with great interest...   and so did some other people.

Later that day Sampson managed to give the parson's sister the slip. The first thing he did after escaping was to get rid of his horrible bow.

He was so absorbed in doing this that he didn't notice the danger until it was too late.

Next day a ransom note arrived at the vicarage.
The parson's sister, upset as she was, was glad to
see the kidnappers had done it correctly,
just like on TV.

We HAVE the cat. Put ALL his Stupendous Winnings! in a Pork bAg and leave in THE NEW statu under the at 10 A.M. tomorrow or YOU will NEVER C him AGAIN.

It will BEANO GOOD telling the POLICE because WE R 2 smart 2 B caught.

Must rush NOW 2 catch THE post. YOURS SINceRely CuRly Dumble CHARLey Numbskill 2 PLANK Street Wortlethorpe

One of his whiskers TO prove THAT we HAVE him

The parson and his sister did exactly what the note
demanded except that they couldn't find a sack big
enough to hold all the cat litter. They did manage to
get in all the flea powder though. They were sad
about the ten pound note but, as they said,
Sampson's life was worth that.

While they were getting the wheelbarrow
Arthur and Humphrey strolled by, and being nosey
they just had to have a peep in the sack.

And before they knew where they were they'd been delivered with the ransom.
They just managed to jump out of the sack before the kidnappers arrived. The first thing they noticed
when they were safe on the ground were some funny Sampson-type noises which they tracked down
while the kidnappers were deciding who should open the sack.

The kidnappers weren't very good at many things, but they were excellent at doing up straps.

The mice were still struggling to undo it when the kidnappers at last got themselves sorted out and made their getaway. The two men were very angry. They knew Sampson had won thousands because they read it in the papers and they weren't going to let him go for a measly ten pounds and some second-hand flea powder.

The mice didn't know exactly what was going on but they did know that their ten pound prize shouldn't be in someone else's pocket.

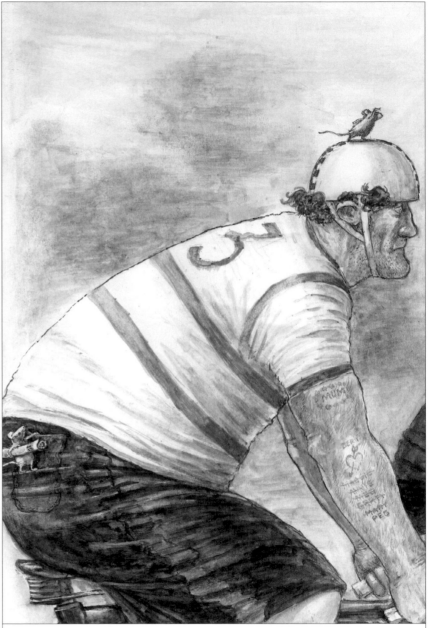

So they removed it. Then Humphrey popped up ahead to see where they were going. But before he had time to find his bearings he lost his footing.

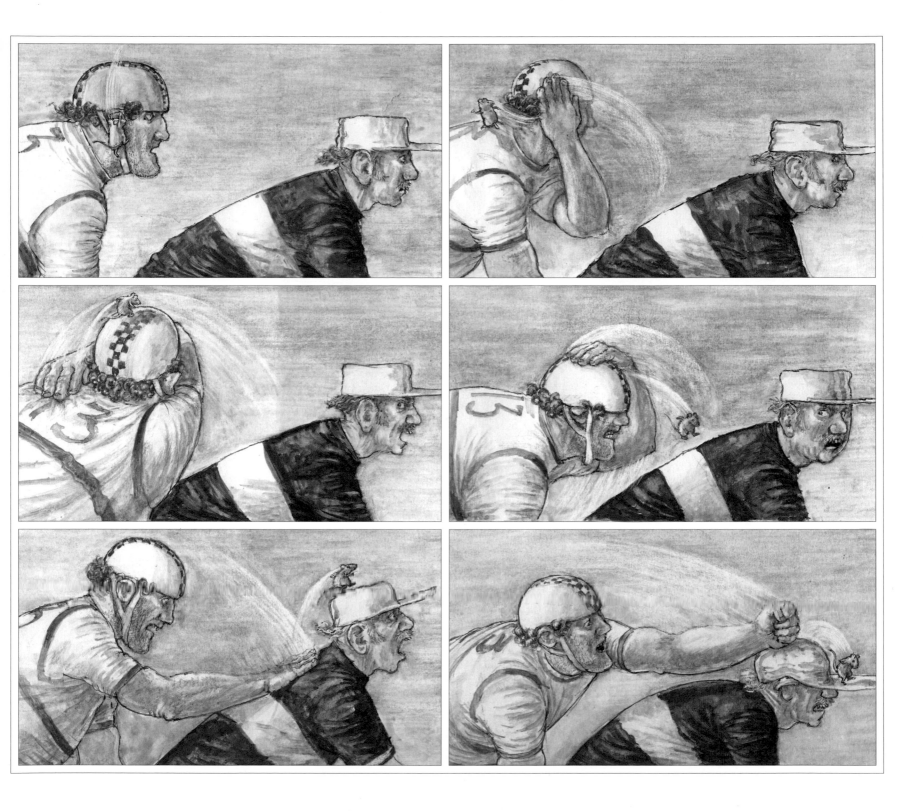

Everybody was still for a while, wondering which bit of himself was broken.
The ten pound note was the first to move, followed closely by Arthur and Humphrey.

The ten pound note had the advantage in the race.

The mice and men were pretty evenly matched.

What the kidnappers gained by length of leg...

the mice made up for by shortness of leg.

Humphrey gasped peevishly that it was disgusting what humans would go through just to get their hands on mere money.

Arthur, wet, puffed, pricked, and stung, just sniffed as sarcastically as shortage of breath would allow.

Then, just when everybody thought the money was within their grasp, their hopes went up in smoke.

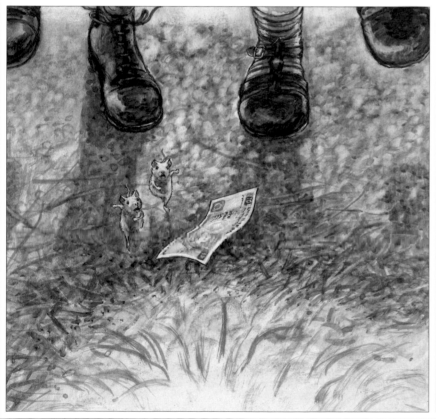

For a few moments everyone's feelings got the better of them. After that the mice set off home.

They would have forgotten all about Sampson if they hadn't come upon the kidnappers again
and stopped to listen to them out of curiosity. Most of the noises the men were making weren't exactly words
but what words they did say were about all the nasty things they were going to do to Sampson,
whom they blamed for all their troubles. At that the mice quickened their pace because they knew
that if Sampson was to get much older they must reach him first.

They did get to Sampson first, but the plastic string around the box was too tough for their teeth.
They just had time to gnaw holes for his legs in the bottom of the box before the kidnappers arrived.

When the kidnappers saw that the box containing Sampson had vanished they did three things.
Firstly, they remembered all the swear words they'd ever known. Secondly, they started to search for the box...

and thirdly, they set an unofficial world tandem speed record over twenty-three miles.

Getting home could have been a problem, but luck was with them. Soon Sampson was unpacked and they were bowling along in comfort. Humphrey suggested that now they had taught the kidnappers that crime didn't pay they could get back to rigging the cat shows and make themselves a fortune. But Arthur and Sampson gave him a look that would have made even a hero's knees knock.

So there were no more cat shows.
A few days later the parson's sister went home
and soon after that the last whiffs of Magnolia
Blossom faded out of Sampson's fur and the mice
stopped holding their noses when they came near
him. The vestry roof leaked more than ever but
the verger kept the stove going day and night
to make up for it.

And with bits of the parish magazine
stuffed in the cracks around the windows
and a few hassocks along the bottom of the doors
to keep out the draughts, the mice could doze
cosily around the stove on winter evenings
while Humphrey told them for the hundredth
time about how he had outwitted
the kidnappers.

THE END

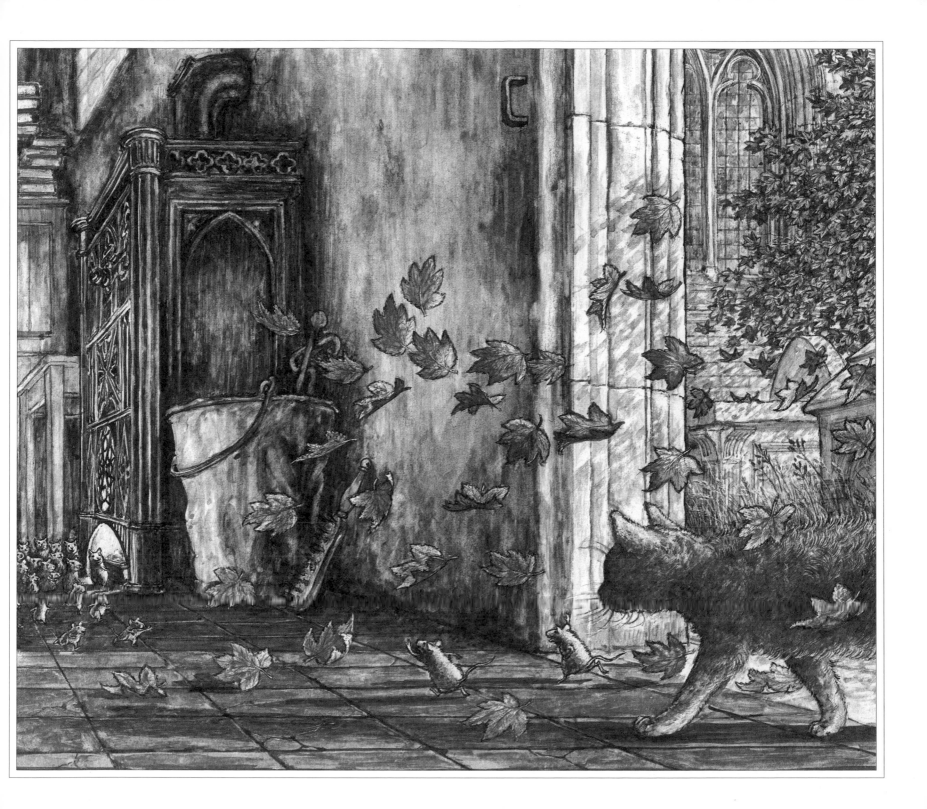

GRAHAM OAKLEY

AND THE CHURCH MICE SERIES

When Graham Oakley began THE CHURCH MOUSE,
he intended to create a series of stories about different public
buildings in Wortlethorpe, but the first book was so
successful that he never got on to the library!

Instead, the stories of Sampson and the church mice became
modern children's classics, garnering critical acclaim and
capturing the imagination of a generation of children.

Between 1972 and 2000, Graham wrote and illustrated
fourteen CHURCH MICE tales. The series was nominated
for two Kate Greenaway Medals, won a *New York Times* Best
Illustrated Children's Book award and sold over one and
a half million books worldwide.